The Fantastic Story of
King Brioche the First

illustrations by Jocelyne Pache
Story by Anne Jenny
Translation by Catherine Barton

Lothrop, Lee & Shepard Co.
New York

For Flox and Zouzou

Once upon a time there was a pretty servant called Nougatine, who cried,

a Fool who didn't play the fool,
a great general, Strategy, who moaned,
a pastrycook, Praline, who spoiled his beautiful rasp-
berry cake with salt tears,

and collapsed in an armchair, a King, Brioche the First,
who no longer cared about anything.

Yet only the evening before, the Fool had made everyone in the palace laugh at his tricks. Brioche the First had ridden proudly on his wheeled horse and had sniffed in delight the marvelous white roses in the royal garden.

Belbobbin, the tailor, had put the last touches to a gorgeous new costume Brioche the First had ordered; and the king, as greedy as he was vain, had stuffed himself with the good things Praline prepared for him.

And in the morning, Brioche the First was still a happy king with no problems. What had happened? While he was walking in his park a little blue bird came and

whispered in his ear, "I am Feather, an ordinary little bird. You are the king. You are happy because you have everything you want . . . but I can fly and you can't."

From that moment Feather never left Brioche the First and never stopped taunting him, "I can fly and you can't! I can fly and you can't!" Perched on the king's cake, Feather helped himself to a cherry. Praline was shocked. He had never seen such cheek! And all the time Feather chanted, "I can fly and you can't! I can fly and you can't!"

Good King Brioche stayed awake all night, wondering how he could fly. Next morning he couldn't even clean his teeth in peace. Feather hopped on his glass. "I can fly and you can't! I can fly and you can't!"

Finally Brioche the First lost his temper and pounced on the little bird, crying, "I am going to put you in a cage. Then you won't be able to fly either, and I shall get some peace!"

General Strategy threatened Feather with even worse punishments to get him to tell the secret of flying.

The servant Nougatine took him out of his cage and gave him tidbits to charm him. "Tell me, dear little bird, how you fly?" But nothing worked, neither threats nor sweets. Poor Feather really didn't *know* how to teach King Brioche the First to fly.

Though Feather was in a cage, the king still had no peace, "Oh! If only I were a bird with big wings," he cried. The Fool, who also longed to help the king, began to flap his arms up and down. "Perhaps this is how you fly?"

Crash! He fell down and hurt himself badly. "What a fool that Fool is!" cried Nougatine.

Suddenly, Brioche the First had an idea. He shut himself up in his study for hours and drew plans for extraordinary machines in which he hoped to be able to fly.

He showed his plans to General Strategy.

"Nonsense," said the general. "Machines like that will never fly!"

Poor Brioche! In the depths of despair, he went back to his own rooms.

Imagine his surprise when he found an enormous cat sitting curled up in his favorite armchair! Throughout the kingdom, this cat was well-known for his size, his greed, and above all, for his magic powers.

"Oh King," he said, "promise me that for the rest of my life I may come to your palace and eat as many cakes as I want, and I will give you a magic spell that will enable you to fly." Overjoyed, the king promised.

The cat handed Brioche four magic cherries and told him to feed them to the little bird. The king, eager to see what would happen, did as the cat said. Then, miraculously, Feather began to grow, and he grew, and grew, and grew until he was changed into a magnificent bird of astounding size.

The king hoisted himself up on Feather's back. Everyone cheered as the two flew off on a marvelous journey,
and Brioche the First's fantastic dream came true at last.

From that day on, the king could often be seen flying over
his kingdom and waving to his subjects.

As for the magical cat, he was often seen in the palace of Brioche the First, licking his lips, his whiskers trembling with pleasure as he sniffed the delicious cakes and other good things that Praline made for him daily.